To Princess Eliza Esmé Haynes
—*K. L.*

To all at Arena with thanks for their support
—*S. H.*

Text copyright © 2014 by Kate Lum
Illustrations copyright © 2014 by Sue Hellard

First published in Great Britain in March 2014 by Bloomsbury Publishing Plc
Published in the United States of America in March 2014
by Bloomsbury Children's Books
www.bloomsbury.com

For information about permission to reproduce selections from this book, write to
Permissions, Bloomsbury Children's Books, 1385 Broadway, New York, New York 10018
Bloomsbury books may be purchased for business or promotional use. For information on bulk
purchases please contact Macmillan Corporate and Premium Sales Department at
specialmarkets@macmillan.com

Library of Congress Cataloging-in-Publication Data
Lum, Kate.
Princesses are not just pretty / by Kate Lum ; illustrated by Sue Hellard. — First U.S. edition.
        pages   cm
Originally published in Great Britain by Bloomsbury Publishing Plc, 2014
Summary: When Princesses Mellie, Allie, and Libby begin to argue about which princess is the prettiest, they decide to hold a contest.
But of course, the girls get sidetracked helping others on their way to the contest, leaving Princess Mellie as the muddiest, Princess Allie
as the yuckiest, and Princess Libby as the drippiest. But due to their kindness, the princesses win in the end.
ISBN 978-1-59990-778-9 (hardcover) • ISBN 978-1-61963-045-1 (reinforced)
[1. Princesses—Fiction. 2. Beauty, Personal—Fiction. 3. Conduct of life—Fiction.] I. Hellard, Susan, illustrator. II. Title.
PZ7.L978705Pn 2014   [E]—dc23   2013025922

Typeset in Garamond • Art created with watercolor

Printed in China by C&C Offset Printing Co., Ltd., Shenzhen, Guangdong
2 4 6 8 10 9 7 5 3 1 (hardcover)
2 4 6 8 10 9 7 5 3 1 (reinforced)

Princesses
Are Not Just Pretty

Kate Lum

illustrated by Sue Hellard

BLOOMSBURY

NEW YORK LONDON NEW DELHI SYDNEY

Once there were three princesses:
Princess Allie, Princess Mellie, and Princess Libby.
They lived in a palace by the sea.
There was always so much to do in the Princessdom,
and the princesses were always very busy.

Now, they were enjoying a well-earned rest under the rose trellis.
"Good work today," said Allie, taking her third cupcake.
"Yup, excellent Princess-ness all around," agreed Libby as she sipped her tea.

"The good thing is," added Mellie,
"we work so hard and we still look
fabulous. I know **I'm** the prettiest,
but **you** look great, too!"

Allie and Libby stared at each other. Then they stared at Mellie. "What do you mean, you're the prettiest?" demanded Allie.

"Oh, nothing," said Mellie. "It's just that someone has to be the prettiest," she added, peering at her reflection in the teapot, "and it happens to be me."

"Actually," sniffed Princess Libby, "I am the prettiest. It's no use denying it. It's my nose, you see—the way it pokes up at the end is just adorable."

"Sorry," interrupted Allie, "but I am the prettiest. It's my freckles, the way they sprinkle my cheeks like cinnamon. Everyone loves cinnamon!"

"As I was saying before I was interrupted," said Mellie, "I am the prettiest. It isn't everyone who has purple hair, you know. It's extra special."

"I am the prettiest," said Allie sharply.

"I am the prettiest," insisted Libby.

"I told you twice, I am the prettiest!" cried Mellie.

Mrs. Blue arrived to clear the trays.

"Mrs. Blue!" cried all the princesses at once, "which of us is the prettiest?"

"Oh dear. Must rush along," said Mrs. Blue.

"WHICH?" demanded the princesses.

"Oh look, is that a squirrel?" asked Mrs. Blue.

"We can't think about anything else until we solve this," said Mellie. "I know: let's have a **beauty contest!**"

"Oh yes!" cried Allie and Libby at once.
"Oh no," said Mrs. Blue.

And so it was decided. The beauty contest would take place that Saturday, and four of the cleverest girls in the land were picked to be the judges.

The day before the contest, Allie, Mellie, and Libby rushed around making themselves as pretty as possible.

Allie gave her hair a special treatment.

Libby bathed in beautifying goo.

Mellie tried on a few dresses.

Then Allie performed
some strengthening exercises.

Libby drank a health potion.

Mellie practiced walking gracefully.

Then . . .
Mellie wrote a victory speech.
Allie developed the perfect curtsy.
Libby tried out an elegant wave.

And . . .

Allie enhanced her freckles
with cinnamon.

Libby scrubbed her tilted nose.

Mellie curled her purple hair.

And they all went to bed and dreamed of being the prettiest.

Early the next morning, Princess Allie got up. She put on her finest gown and set off for the contest.

As she passed the palace bakery, however, she smelled something strange. She poked her head inside and gasped—smoke!

Thick smoke was pouring from the ovens.

The servants had gone to see the contest and forgotten the royal bread.

Allie grabbed a hose and sprang into action. **WHOOSH!**

Meanwhile, Libby put on her loveliest
gown and marched out, nose first, to the contest.
But as she passed the park, she heard a sound.

"Help! Oh no! Help me-e-e!" It was
coming from the duck pond.

Libby raced over, just in time to see a little girl
wade into the deep mud by the side of the water.

"My kitty fell in!
He can't swim!"
cried the little girl.
"I can swim!" called
Libby. And she did.
SPLASH!

Meanwhile, Princess Mellie was ready for the contest. She strolled out, thinking her hair had never looked purpler. But as she walked along the lane, she heard a small voice shouting.

"Pigs! Pigs!
Get back here, pigs!
Pig alert! Wa-a-a-a-i-t!"
Past her feet ran a line of piglets, followed by a small boy in a muddy shirt.

"Help, Princess!" he shouted.
"My pigs!"
And so, she helped. **SPLAT!**

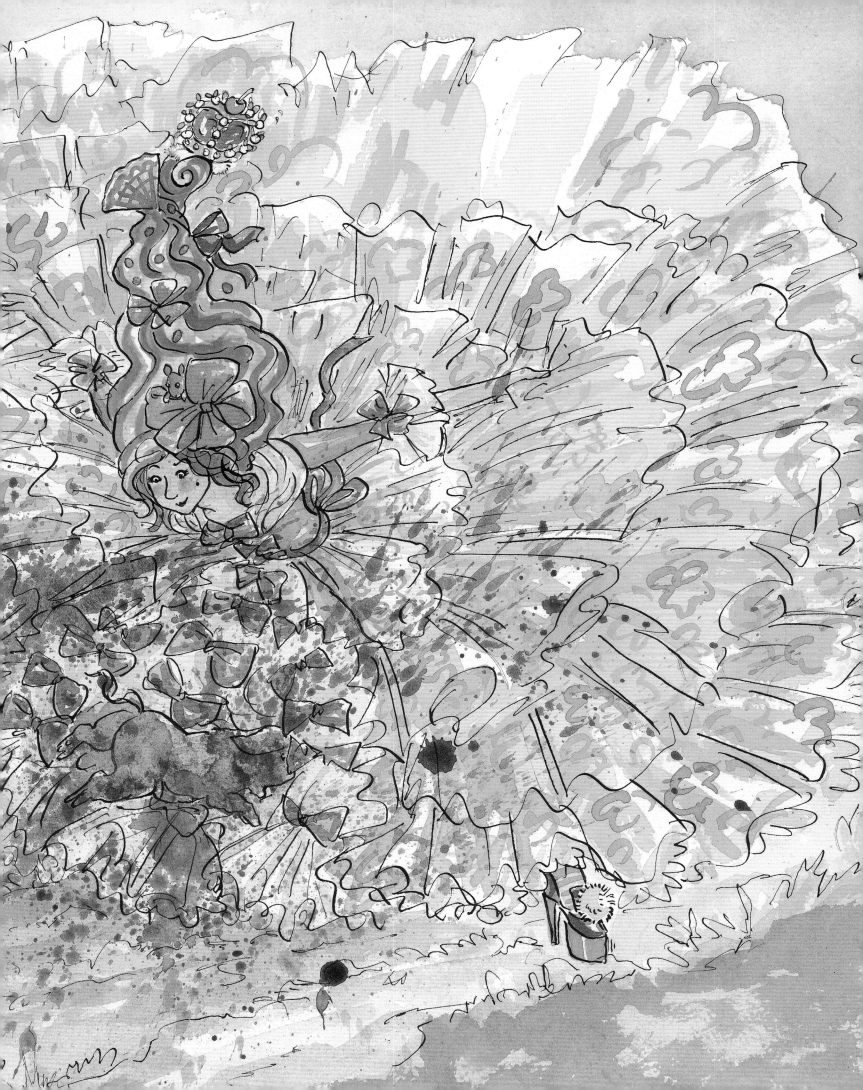

Meanwhile, at the contest hall, people were getting restless.
Mrs. Blue tried to help. She sang a few songs.
She played the accordion. She even performed a dance.
But where, oh where, were the princesses?

At last, the Royal Page blew his trumpet. "The Princesses have arrived!" he announced.
The curtains parted, and all the people sat up, eager to see their Royal Prettinesses.

One by one, they stepped onto the stage. Princess Allie came first. She looked . . . **remarkable**.

Princess Libby came next. She looked . . . **incredible**.

Princess Mellie came last. She looked . . . **unforgettable**.

The audience whispered as the judges wrote on their scorecards. At last, the smallest judge stood on her chair.

"We hereby announce our decision," she read. "Of all the Princesses ever seen in the land:

Princess Allie is
the yuckiest!

Princess Libby is
the drippiest!

And Princess Mellie is the muddiest!

You have **all** shown us that **princesses are not just pretty!**"

"Three cheers for the Best Princesses!" cried all the people.